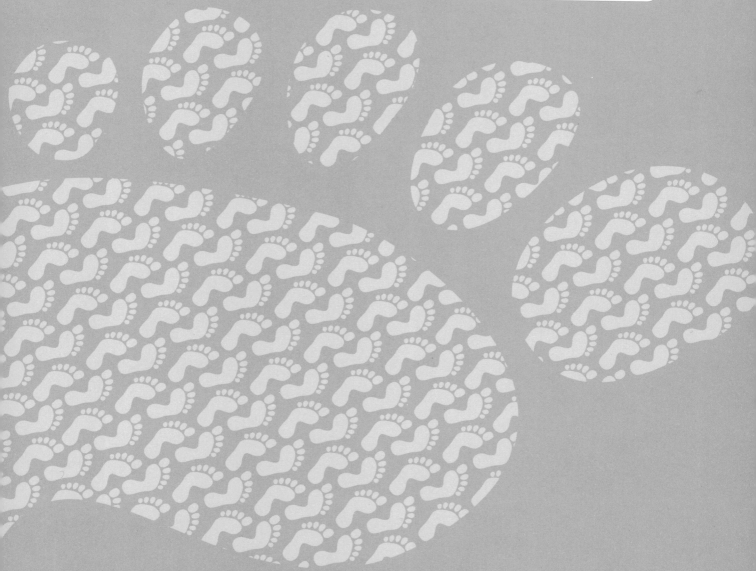

Why Should I Care About Nature?

one small step

M J Knight

A⁺
Smart Apple Media

Smart Apple Media is published by Black Rabbit Books
P.O. Box 3263, Mankato, Minnesota 56002

Printed in China

Library of Congress Cataloging-in-Publication Data

Knight, M. J. (Mary-Jane)
    Why should I care about nature? / M.J. Knight.
    p. cm. — (Smart Apple Media. One small step)
    Summary: "Facts about how pollution harms nature and practical
tips for kids about how they can contribute to protecting natural
habitats"—Provided by publisher.
    ISBN 978-1-59920-266-2 (hardcover)
    1. Habitat (Ecology)—Juvenile literature. 2. Habitat
conservation—Juvenile literature. 3. Nature—Juvenile literature. I.
Title.
QH541.14.K58 2009
333.95'16—dc22

                                                    2008011372

Designed by Guy Callaby
Edited by Jinny Johnson
Illustrations by Hel James
Picture research by Su Alexander

Picture acknowledgements
Title page Paulo De Oliveira/OSF; 4 Craig Tuttle/Corbis; 8 Juniors
Bildarchiv/OSF; 10 Paulo De Oliveira/OSF; 11 Juniors Bildarchiv/
OSF; 12 OSF; 14 David Tipling/OSF; 15 Colin McPherson/Corbis;
16 Martyn Colbeck/OSF; 17 Mike Powles/OSF; 18 Pacific Stock/
OSF; 21 Paul A Souders/Corbis; 22 Charles Philip Cangialosi/Corbis;
23 Joson/Zefa/Corbis; 24 Michael Leach/OSF; 27 Reg Charity/
Corbis; 28 Martin Jones/Corbis
Front cover: Dietrich Roze/Zefa/Corbis

9 8 7 6 5 4 3 2 1

Contents

Somewhere to Live

Everyone has to live somewhere, and that goes for animals as well as human beings.

The place where a plant or an animal lives is called a habitat. Living things find food and shelter in their habitats.

There are hundreds of different habitats all around the world. There are habitats in your yard or local park and in your school grounds.

These black-tailed deer live on the edge of the forest in Mount Rainier National Park, Washington, U.S. They feed on plants.

One Small Fact

Forests cover about 30 percent of the world's land.

Why Are Habitats Important?

Each habitat is home to particular types of plants and animals. If everything is left undisturbed, the wildlife in the habitat is balanced. But if something happens to change that balance, the plants and animals that live there might be damaged or even die. That is why it is so important not to disturb natural habitats.

Ladybugs live in gardens, meadows, shrubs, and fields in many different parts of the world.

A Step in the Right Direction

You might think that what you do does not matter, but it matters very much. Every time you think about the plants and animals that live around you or elsewhere in the world, you are making a difference. Everyone can make a difference, and if lots of people choose to do this, they will make a very big difference.

Who Eats Who?

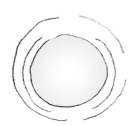

All living things need food to give them energy to grow. A food chain is a way of showing who eats who in a habitat.

Food chains always start with a plant. Plants make their own food. They use energy from the sun and the chlorophyll in their green leaves. They take water from the ground through their roots and carbon dioxide gas from the air through their leaves. This way of making food is called photosynthesis.

A food chain in water

Plants grow in a pond or stream and make their food by photosynthesis.

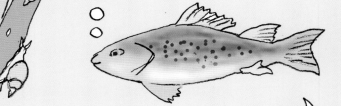

Fish eat the pond snails and some plants.

Pond snails eat the plants.

Animals cannot make their own food. Some get their energy by eating plants. Other animals get their energy by eating the animals that eat the plants. They are all part of a food chain.

Birds catch fish and eat them.

Birds eat dragonflies too. Dragonflies also feed on other insects that they catch in the air.

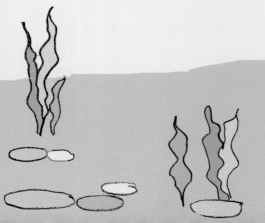

Young dragonflies eat water insects, tadpoles, and even small fish.

One Small Fact

If plants could not turn the sun's energy into food, we would all die. We can eat all sorts of plants and their seeds and fruits, but we cannot eat sunshine. Plants are vital to life on our planet.

Links in a Chain

Lots of food chains joined together make a food web.

A food chain follows just one path as animals find food. At the bottom of a food chain might be grass, which a grasshopper eats. Then a frog might eat the grasshopper. A snake might eat the frog and an owl might eat the snake.

A food web shows many more links than a chain. For example, an owl might eat a mouse or a squirrel as well as a snake. A snake might eat a caterpillar or a beetle, and a frog might eat a slug or a fly.

Rabbits eat grass and other plants. Predators such as buzzards and foxes hunt and eat rabbits.

At the top of every food chain and food web are animals called predators. Predators eat other animals, called prey. In the middle of every food chain and food web are the prey animals, which other animals eat. Prey animals eat plants. At the bottom of every food web are plants.

A Food Web

Snails, grasshoppers, and mice eat the grass at the bottom of this web. Frogs eat snails and grasshoppers. Snakes eat frogs, grasshoppers, snails, and mice. Owls are at the top of this food web. They eat all the other animals.

What Can Go Wrong?

If just one animal is missing from a food chain or a food web, it makes a big difference to the entire web.

Think about the food chain on the previous page. A grasshopper eats grass, a frog eats the grasshopper, a snake eats the frog, and an owl eats the snake. What do you think would happen if you took the frog out of the food chain?

This barn owl is at the top of a food chain. Barn owls hunt and eat mice, small rodents, and shrews.

If There Were No Frogs...

1. There would be more and more grasshoppers because there are no frogs to eat them.

2. There would be less and less grass because more grasshoppers are eating it.

3. When they have eaten all the grass, the grasshoppers have no more food, so they die.

4. If there are no frogs, the snakes must look somewhere else for food.

5. If there are no snakes, the owls must look for food somewhere else too.

The food chain has been broken, and the habitat the animals live in changes.
Find out why on the next page.

Grasshopper Facts

● There are about 5,000 different types of grasshoppers living around the world. They live in marshes, deserts, rain forests, and fields.

● Grasshoppers eat grass and plants. They can be pests to farmers when they eat farm crops.

● Grasshoppers protect themselves from enemies by jumping or flying away. They can bite their enemies with their strong jaws.

Grasshoppers are food for several animals in the food chain. Their strong back legs help them to leap away from danger.

Breaking the Chain

Why do you think frogs might disappear from a food chain?

Frogs like to live in ponds and streams and damp places. Ponds are often filled in so houses or roads can be built on the land. The frogs lose their habitat. People sometimes throw trash into ponds or pollute them with chemicals, and frogs die. The death of the frogs has a big effect on the whole food web in the area.

The trash that people have thrown into this pond makes it difficult for wild animals to live here.

One Small Fact

In the past 10 years, up to 170 species of frogs have become extinct.

Frogs help gardeners by eating the slugs and snails that damage their plants.

Frogs need water when they lay their eggs, which turn into tadpoles. But most of the time, frogs live on land. They are very useful to gardeners because they love to eat slugs, snails, and insects. Keep a damp patch in your garden, and see if you can encourage a frog to visit.

I Can Make a Difference

Do you have a pond in your yard, or are there any ponds near where you live? Ask your parents to help you find out whether there is a pond in your nearest wild area. FrogWatch USA (http://www.nwf.org/frogwatchusa/) relies on volunteers to count frog populations.

Why Do Habitats Change?

Habitats change for many reasons. One reason is that there are so many people on Earth and they all need somewhere to live. Another reason is that people want to use something that grows in a habitat.

Many types of animals live at all levels of this tropical rain forest in the Amazon Basin in South America.

Who Lives in the Rain Forests?

More than 5 million species of plants and animals

More than 50 million people

In some places, this can cause many problems for wildlife. Some areas with particular problems are the rain forests in South America, Africa, and Asia.

Rain forests cover a tiny bit of Earth, yet more than half of all living things live there. In a rain forest, trees grow close together, forming a canopy over the ground. Under the trees, it is dark and damp and many animals live there.

I Can Make a Difference

FSC

You can help protect the rain forests by helping to make sure your family buys furniture with the letters FSC on it. They stand for the Forest Stewardship Council, which makes sure that taking the wood for furniture does not damage the rain forest.

The problems start when people cut down the trees—to make room for roads, houses or fields, or to turn the trees into furniture or paper. Every time trees are cut down, there are fewer trees for forest birds and animals to live in and feed on. So we need to try to protect these precious forests.

People have cut down the rain forest trees to make fields so they can grow crops in this part of the Amazon.

Room for Everyone?

People are changing natural habitats all over the world.

Many animals suffer when people take the land they live on. Mountain gorillas and chimpanzees have lost their living space in Africa and so have orangutans in Indonesia and Malaysia.

Another animal that has lost living space is the elephant. Elephants need lots of space to roam around and find food. That can be difficult in some African countries where people are turning more wild land into fields.

This African elephant has plenty of space to roam and find food near Mount Kilimanjaro in Africa.

One Small Fact

African elephants are the largest land animals and weigh up to 14,000 lbs. (6,350 kg).

16

In China, the giant panda is endangered because so much of the land it lived on has been taken over by farmers. Pandas eat only bamboo and, like elephants, they need to eat lots of food every day to survive. So when they lose land, they lose food too.

These species and many others around the world are listed as endangered. This means that everyone needs to do whatever they can to keep them from dying out altogether.

There are now probably only about 1,600 giant pandas left living in the wild in China.

I Can Make a Difference

You can help protect endangered animals by joining a group, such as the World Wildlife Fund, which helps to set up protected areas for wildlife. There are also groups that help individual animals. The Dian Fossey Gorilla Fund gives you the chance to adopt a gorilla. Perhaps you could organize some fund-raising activities at home or at school and collect enough money to help a gorilla or other endangered animals.

Underwater Wildlife

There are lots of habitats under the sea.

Fiji is a country in the South Pacific that has more than 300 islands. Thousands of colorful tropical fish live in the sea around the islands. Its long coral reef is also home to whales, dolphins, sharks, turtles, fish, and giant clams. Scientists discover new species on the reef that no one has heard of before.

The fan-shaped fins on the lionfish look like a lion's mane. It is hunting for food by a coral reef in the South Pacific Ocean.

The problem in Fiji is that people have caught too many of the fish that live there. Sometimes people break off pieces of the coral reef too.

The good news is that in a few years there will be an area where all the wildlife will be protected. This will be the largest underwater sanctuary (safe place) in the world. No one will be allowed to catch fish there so the fish will be able to breed and they will not die out. Other creatures on the reef will be safe too.

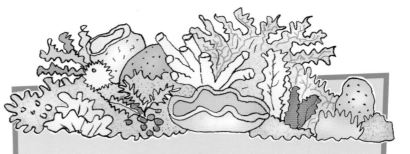

Coral Facts

● A reef is made up of many tiny coral animals living close together. Each animal has a hard stony skeleton. These are left behind when the coral animal dies and become part of the coral reef.

● Coral reefs can be thousands of years old.

● More different kinds of fish live in a coral reef than anywhere else in the sea.

I Can Make a Difference

A group called the Marine Stewardship Council (MSC) wants everyone to eat fish that is caught without harming other sea animals. Help your parents look for the blue MSC label when you buy fresh or canned fish. Find out more on the MSC Web site listed on page 31.

The Last Wilderness

A wilderness is a wild place that has not been changed by the activities of people. Do you know where the biggest wilderness in the world is? It is Antarctica.

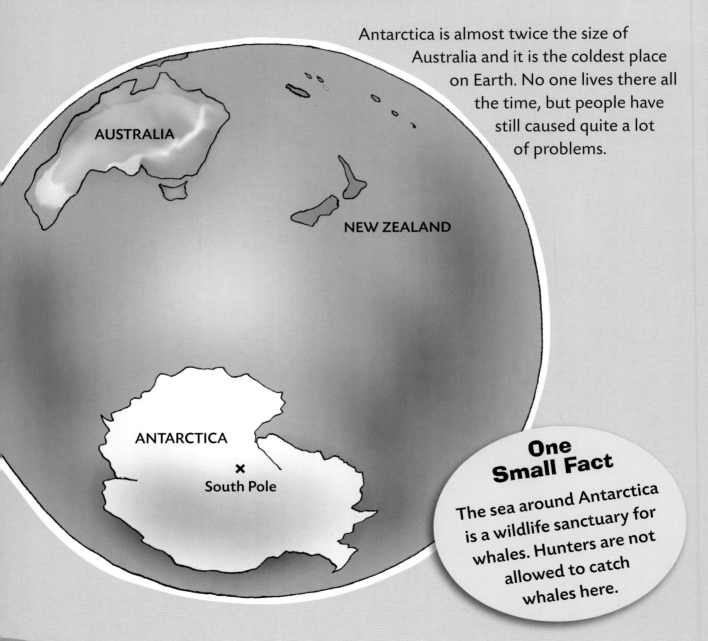

Antarctica is almost twice the size of Australia and it is the coldest place on Earth. No one lives there all the time, but people have still caused quite a lot of problems.

AUSTRALIA

NEW ZEALAND

ANTARCTICA

× South Pole

One Small Fact

The sea around Antarctica is a wildlife sanctuary for whales. Hunters are not allowed to catch whales here.

There is a lot of wildlife in the seas around Antarctica—hundreds of different fish and amazing seabirds, such as albatross and penguins. There are also huge elephant seals. Many of the animals eat a tiny shrimp called krill. Fish and squid eat the krill, then seals, penguins, and other seabirds eat the fish. Some whales eat krill too.

There are rules about who can fish in the Antarctic seas and how much fish they can catch. But some fishermen catch fish even when they are not allowed. Some catch krill to feed fish grown in fish farms. This damages the food chain. If there is not enough krill, animals that depend on it will die.

Blue Whales

● The blue whale is the world's biggest mammal and eats 40 million krill every day.

Antarctic krill are usually about this size.

● Blue whales can live up to 110 years.

● There may be fewer than 2,000 blue whales left in the world.

Penguins and other creatures are being harmed by the large amounts of garbage dumped in Antarctica.

Wildlife at Risk

There are laws that help stop wild animals from being caught or killed, but not everyone obeys them.

In Africa, hunters called poachers kill black rhinos to take their horns. Rhino horns are used in some Chinese medicines. Poachers also kill elephants for their tusks. The tusks are made into jewelry and carvings.

Some birds, such as parrots and macaws, are caught in the wild and then sold as pets. The hunters transport them in dangerous ways, so they sometimes die before they ever become anyone's pet.

The black rhinoceros is an endangered species because so many have been killed for their horns.

One Small Fact

There are fewer than 4,000 black rhinos left in the wild in Africa.

Some snakes and lizards are caught and sold as pets too. Others may be killed for their beautiful skins. In some countries, sea turtles are killed for their shells or because people want to eat them.

Sometimes lizards are killed so that bags, belts, or shoes can be made from their beautiful skins.

I Can Make a Difference

If your family goes on vacation to another country, think about the souvenirs you might bring back. Some souvenirs are illegal. They could be ornaments or jewelry made from ivory (elephants' tusks) or clothes made from the skins of lizards and snakes, such as belts or shoes.

If your family wants to buy a pet such as a bird, snake, or lizard, make sure it comes from a store that looks after its animals properly and does not buy from people who break the law.

Closer to Home

You can do a lot to help the wildlife that lives nearer to home.

Wherever you live, there will be a wildlife habitat near you that you can help to look after. If you have a garden, look at what grows there, and see whether you can spot any insects, spiders, centipedes, etc. Even if you only have a balcony, you can attract birds by hanging up a bird feeder or putting up a nest box.

Bird feeders will attract small birds.

If your family has a garden, even if it is small, you can help make space for wildlife. Try leaving an old log to rot in a corner with some dead leaves to make a cozy home for beetles and spiders.

I Can Make a Difference

Join a wildlife trust. These are organizations that look after the wildlife in different areas. They have events and activities for children of all ages, as well as families, and are always glad to find new members who want to learn about wildlife and how to look after it.

Wildlife at School

Does your school have a garden? If so, you could get together with some friends and help turn it into a wildlife garden.

If your school has any kind of outdoor area, you can think about ways to attract wildlife. Start by asking your teacher whether you can do a survey of the grounds.

School Grounds Survey

Trees How many trees? What type? How big? Can you guess how old they are? Can you spot any birds or insects?

Hedges Are there hedges or fences around the grounds? Do trees or bushes grow there? Are there wild flowers? Can you spot any birds or insects?

Grass Is there a grassy area or field? How big? Are there wild flowers? Can you spot any birds or insects?

Pond Do you have a pond or damp places? What can you see there?

Flowers Do you have a flower garden? Which flowers grow there? Can you see any birds or animals?

Compost heap Does your school have one? What grows around it? Can you see any creatures there?

I Can Make a Difference

You can encourage insects to visit by building a bug hotel. Tie a few twigs or bamboo canes together and hang them under a tree branch or fence. Then watch to see who visits. You could also cut the bottom off an old plastic bottle, fill it with damp leaves, and see what happens.

Make a Wildlife Garden

When you have finished your survey, talk about what you could do next.

Can you think of ways to make the grounds better for the wildlife in them? Could you set up a wildlife club and ask parents and family to help after school or on weekends?

If you have space to make a pond in your wildlife garden, many animals, birds, and insects will come and live there.

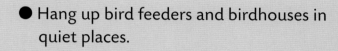

I Can Make a Difference

To encourage wildlife:

● Hang up bird feeders and birdhouses in quiet places.

● Leave dead logs in a corner to encourage insects such as pill bugs to live there.

● Plant some trees or flowers to encourage bees and butterflies (find out which ones they like best).

● Plant some shrubs and bushes to cover the ground and give small animals shelter and shade.

● Start a compost heap.

You can find more information and ideas for doing these things on the Web sites listed on page 31.

Look up information about plants and animals in the school library or on the computer. Can you find out more about the wildlife you have already? Can you think of ways to encourage more wildlife to visit?

Glossary

Antarctica
The area of land and sea around the South Pole.

compost
Decayed plant and food waste that can be turned into plant food.

endangered
An animal in a harmful or dangerous situation. Without help, endangered animals may disappear from Earth altogether.

food chain
A series of living things linked together because each one feeds on another in the chain. Food chains always start with a plant and end with a predator.

food web
A connected set of food chains.

habitat
The place where a plant or an animal lives.

mammal
A warm-blooded animal, usually with four legs and some hair on its body. Female mammals feed their babies with milk from their own bodies. Cats, dogs, and humans are all mammals.

photosynthesis
The way green plants make their food using water, carbon dioxide, sunshine, and chlorophyll from their leaves.

poacher
Someone who breaks the law by killing or taking animals illegally.

predator
An animal that hunts and eats other animals.

prey
Animals that are hunted and eaten by other animals.

tropical rain forest
A dense forest in parts of the world called the tropics where the weather is very warm and wet.

Web Sites

http://www.wildlifetrusts.org/
Use this Web site to find your nearest wildlife trust.

http://www.nwf.org/backyard/
Learn how to create a wildlife habitat in your backyard.

http://www.worldwildlife.org/
The Explore section of the World Wildlife Fund's Web site has games and info.

http://www.gorillafund.org/
Information about gorillas and how you can help them.

http://www.nationalgeographic.com/geographyaction/habitats/explore.html
The games and activities on this Web site explore habitats and endangered species.

http://eng.msc.org/html/content_527.htm
Information about fish and how it is caught. It has lots of games and fun for kids too at **http://www.fishandkids.org/**

http://www.pbs.org/wnet/nature/orangutans/index.html
Learn how the intelligent orangutan uses tools.

Index